Spooky Cat

C.H. Lyn

Contents

Contents

Other Works by C.H. Lyn

<u>Spooky Cat Stories</u>
One Hell of a Road Trip (2)
Spelling Disaster (3)
<u>The Abredea Series</u>
Hope and Lies
Truth and Fury
<u>Miss Belle's Travel Guides</u>
Lacey Goes to Tokyo
Damen Goes to Peru
<u>The Old Tales</u>
Song of the Deep
A Voice in the Tower
<u>Works with Tracey Barski</u>
Love is Murder
Secrets of the Unborn: The Leader & The Rebel Duology

Content Warning

- Light visual horror

- Non-binary-phobia

- Mild language

- Harassment

- Blood/Self-harm in the context of a ritual

One

My parents taught me to say "bless you" when someone sneezes, but it was Nana who told me why.

Being a kid, I laughed off her warnings. Sneezing doesn't open the door for demons, and not just because demons aren't real but because that notion is ridiculous. Or... it was.

I kept it up. Doing the polite thing long after I fell out of the habit of going to church. Little old lady on the bus? *Bless you*. Three-year-old at the grocery store? *Bless you*. Bald monk at the farmer's market? *Bless you*.

But my cat? The tiny stray who wound up in my apartment as a favor for a friend, and ended up staying because she's good at keeping a low profile when the landlord comes around?

I guess being cooped up for a year broke me of the habit.

• • • ● ● • ● ● • ● • •

My miniscule black cat is standing on the sill, one paw raised in the air, staring. Not at me, but at the apartment. Her gaze—no longer a moonlight yellow, but red and glinting—takes it all in. As though she's never seen it before.

The room grows cold.

"Missy…" I murmur.

Her head twitches. Flicks my direction and those red eyes look me head on.

My breath catches in my throat. My heartbeat pounds through my ears. Slowly, Missy steps from her basket, walks along the windowsill, and jumps onto the tiny kitchen table, her gaze fixed on me the whole time.

A demonic voice chills me to the bone as it says, "*Missy?*"

My cat's mouth doesn't move, but I know it's coming from her. From the way she stares at me, red eyes fixed on my brown ones. I hear the icy tone as though she'd spoken right next to my ear.

"*That's a stupid name.*"

A flash of irritation. I raise an eyebrow at the thing that has taken over my cat. My fingers go to the thick chords of black wrapped around my wrist. I fiddle with the gold and silver beads dangling from the leather.

"It's better than Moony." My voice is sure, stronger than it feels in my throat. "That's what they called her before she came to me."

A snort. Didn't know cats could snort.

"*I suppose it is better.*" The red gaze leaves me for a moment. Surveys its own paws. Claws—filed down a few days ago—protract and retract a few times.

I swallow.

"*What is this?*"

I walk slowly from the kitchen counter to the chair on the far side of the table from not-Missy. I sink into my wobbly seat and take a sip from my coffee, trying for nonchalant.

"What do you mean?"

"*This creature.*" Not-Missy looks up at me. "*What is it?*"

"It's…" I squint and cock my head to the side. "How are you in something without knowing what it is?"

I recognize the nose-twitch. It's the same one the real Missy does when I'm late with her breakfast. Or when I've used the can-opener for something besides her occasional tuna treat.

"*A door opened, and I went through,*" the icy voice hisses. "*Circumstances prevented me from being overly picky.*"

I nod like I understand and raise my mug to my lips. I'm proud of the lack of hand trembling as I say, "Missy is a cat."

Not-Missy blinks. They inhale. They let out a yowl that drives instinct through my cool demeanor.

I jerk back from the table and scramble to put several feet between me and the creature rolling around on the tabletop. Coffee spills from the edge of my mug. A ring forms around the pale ceramic.

"*No, no, no,*" echoes through my head.

"What…" I swallow and take another step back, my fingers moving toward a knife on the counter. At the same time, my gut churns at the thought of hurting Missy. "What are *you?*"

Not-Missy—still yowling—falls off the table. They land on their side and glare up at me from the floor. Those red eyes seem to pierce my soul.

"I'm a being of shadow. Of horror and fear. Of fury and darkness. I'm a sneeze demon. Obviously."

The incredulity in their voice sends another flutter of irritation down my spine. I rest my hand on my hip. My instinctual self-preservation calms at the halt in yowling.

A snicker escapes my nose as I roll the words around in my mind. "A... sneeze demon?"

"Yes," the thing snaps. *"Technically I'd be called a shadow demon, but I came across via a sneeze, which makes me a sneeze demon."* Not-Missy glowers down at their paws. *"I can't believe I waited five-hundred years for this chance and now I'm a cat. This is ridiculous."*

Two

"What were you expecting?"

"*A human. Or at least a dog or something. I hate cats.*"

Now, I'll pause the story here to say while I was lightly offended by this, I also saw an opportunity. And, wanting Missy back, I took it.

I move away from the knife, rip the last of the paper towels from the roll, and give the demon a wide berth as I cross back to the table to clean up my spill. "Is... uh. Is there any way to get you *out* of Missy so you can... try again, I guess?"

The demon squints, tilting Missy's head, and watching me with those glowing red eyes. "*You'd... you'd be willing to perform an exorcism?*"

"If that's what it takes, sure." I shrug, a handful of soggy, sticky paper towels in my hand. I toss them into the trashcan and rinse the bean-water off my fingers. "I don't have a lot going on today."

The eyes glint with excitement.

A shudder runs down my spine as not-Missy slinks forward. They get to the kitchen tile and leap onto the counter. The movement is familiar but hauntingly different. Like a deer walking after getting hit by a car.

Sitting with a rigid back and wide eyes, they survey me.

I resist the urge to spray them with the sink hose. Something tells me this *thing* won't react the same way Missy does when I chase her out of the kitchen.

I take a step back, finding the edge of the yellow laminate counter blocking my way. I hold up a hand. "Hang on a sec. What's to stop you from possessing me... if I get you out of my cat?"

Not-Missy's little black ears droop slightly, and they do the nose twitch again. "*I'd have to promise it. And you'd have to not sneeze.*"

I raise my eyebrow, the one with a studded sapphire piercing.

Not-Missy sighs. "*Are there others in the area at least?*"

"Dogs?"

"*People.*"

I nod. A weight pulls at my chest. "Right. Yeah. It's an apartment complex in a big city. Lots of people."

The cat nods. An unsettling sight. "*I've been gone from the mortal plane for some time. Are most as impolite as you these days?*"

"What?" I snap, indignant.

Not-Missy gestures with a paw. Also unsettling. "*Not saying the... well, the magic words?*"

I roll my eyes and heave a sigh. "You sound like my Nana." I run a hand across the cropped haircut I've been playing with. A rainbow of color hides the remaining brown. I dye it one piece at a time when I get bored. "I usually say it. But no, not everyone does. There's a drug dealer on the first floor. I doubt anyone tells him 'bless you'."

Not-Missy flinches. I make a mental note of the reaction.

"I'm just saying," I continue. "He could use a personality shift, if I'm being honest."

"*Hmm.*" The cat raises a paw to its chin. "*I'd excel at selling drugs.*"

I choke on my own spit and cough out a laugh. "Not quite what I meant, but sure."

Maybe not the most moral thing I've ever done, but Missy is my gal. My buddy. My cute mangy cat who curls up in my lap while I'm watching TV or sleeping.

It's been a lonely year. I want my friend back.

The apartment is quiet for a moment, save the sounds of the city outside the open window. Car horns, engines, pigeons and gulls fighting over scraps, and the constant clanging of construction a few blocks away.

Still, it feels like silence compared to not-Missy's hissing in my head.

A frown creases my brow. "What do I call you?"

The demon pauses mid paw-lick. Red eyes survey me. "*I'm a demon.*"

"Yes." I fold my arms across my loose-knit sweater. "That's been established. I mean, what's your name?"

They blink. Once, twice, three times as they stare at me. I suppose I've seen alarm on Missy's face before, but this isn't quite that.

"I... you can call me Skia."

I nod. "Cool. Skia. I like it."

"And what... what are you?"

There's a question. One my parents and relatives have asked too many times for it to be confusion anymore.

I shake it off. That's not what the demon is asking. "Demi. You can call me, Demi. Now." I unfold my arms and clap my hands together. The sound reverberates through the apartment. As many plants and rugs as I have, the space is still empty enough for echoes. "How do I get you out of my cat?"

Skia jumps from the counter to the ledge a few feet away. It splits the room, bisecting the kitchen from the small couch and dining space. Standing atop, Skia eyes my drooping spider plants for a moment before looking down at the floor below.

"You'll need to move these things." A tiny paw gestures to the couch and carpets. *"We need a clear floor to work with. Maybe give it a mop. Skin cells will affect the ritual."*

I can't decide which part of that freaks me out. Probably the demon-cat exorcism part... but thinking about my skin cells all over the floor isn't great either.

"What else? I've got a few candles, and a couple of..." My mouth twists to the side, and I raise a shoulder in half a shrug, knowing I'm about to feel stupid. "Crystals in some of the plants."

Skia scoffs. Not in my head either, a full-on cat scoff.

I glower.

"No. None of that will help. Unless your candles are fresh, eight inches tall, and white?"

My teeth click with annoyance. "Nope."

"Very well. We shall have to visit an apothecary."

I open my mouth, close it again, and squint up at the demon. After a moment I hesitantly ask, "When was the last time you were here, again?"

"Five-hundred years ago, give or take. Why? Do humans no longer sell candles, chalk, herbs?"

"We do... it's just..." I scratch my forehead. "Never mind. I'll make a list. You can wait here, and I'll pick up whatever we need. In a couple hours you'll be out, and I'll have Missy back."

"Oh, I'm going with you, Demi. I'll not risk my presence on the mortal plane on you mistaking baby's breath for nightshade."

I open my mouth to object, realize I have no idea what baby's breath or nightshade look like, and give a begrudging nod. "Fine. Let me move this," I gesture to the small coffee table and the russet carpet underneath it, "and then we'll get going."

Three

I scribble Skia's list down on an old pad of DC Superhero themed sticky-notes.

"*No,*" Skia hisses, swatting at my hand. "*Black chalk. Black. Get the details right.*"

"Can't I use white chalk?" I ask, exasperated.

"*No. White chalk is for bodies. Black chalk is for rituals.*"

"How do you..." I squint, sigh, and shake my head. "Never mind. What else?"

"*I do believe that's it.*" Skia pads across the table.

I lean back as the demon gets too close for comfort. It's doing the thing Missy does when I try to read.

"*Yes. This is it. Let's go.*"

"Hang on." I scoot back from the table. "We can't just go out with you looking... well." I fidget with my hands. "You've got glowing red eyes, Skia."

"*And?*"

"That's not exactly... Most creatures don't have glowing red eyes. It might attract unwanted attention."

"Unwanted for whom?"

I hesitate here, scrambling for a reason that won't offend. "You don't want people saying—you know, the magic words. If they spot a demon running around, they might be more careful than usual."

"Indeed," Skia nods, *"and we wouldn't want you burned at the stake before you finish the ritual."*

"Right. Yeah, that, too."

"Well then, human—"

"Demi."

A cat eye roll. *"Demi. What do you propose?"*

I frown, click my teeth a couple times and play with the dangling pieces on my bracelet. The solution comes to me, and a flutter of fear goes through my stomach.

I look at the demon-cat. "You're not gonna like this."

Skia gestures a paw up and down Missy's chest and face. *"Way ahead of you."*

I shrug. Then I go to the open closet next to my bed and rifle through a few boxes at the top.

"Here we go," I mutter, pulling a contact lens case from between a pair of fangs and pointed ear prosthetics.

"What is that?"

"Missy has yellow eyes... usually." I cross to the table and gesture for Skia to move closer. "I went as a vampire fairy last time they had a renaissance faire in the area."

"I understand all of those words but none of the context."

I laugh, and Skia raises an eyebrow.

"Just come here and try to hold still. I have contacts to put in your eyes. They'll make it harder to tell that my cat is possessed by a demon."

Skia gives a rumbling growl that I assume is approval and plants themself right in front of me.

I unscrew the contact case, rinse off the first one, and glance at the cat that is a demon but also still a cat. "This is gonna feel weird, but hold still and it'll be done real fast."

I lean forward, one hand holding Missy's soft head while my pointer finger steadily approaches her eye. Skia flinches, jerks a bit, but I hold firm and...

"Ouch!" I wince back, the chair scraping against the ground in my hurry to move away from a bloody set of claws. Three angry lines of red mark my right forearm. Blood oozes, and I hurry to the sink to rinse out the cuts.

"What the *hell* was that?"

"*The cat is not pleased.*"

I squint and then grimace as I pump soap onto the scrapes, rubbing it in. A groan escapes my lips before I glance at the demon. "What?"

Skia glares with one yellow eye and one red one.

At least the contact went in.

"*Your cat is still here. Inside. And she's not pleased.*"

The anger fades, though the water still running across my arm stings like crazy. "Missy is like... aware?"

"*Somewhat. She's a cat, Demi. She's as aware as usual.*"

My chest constricts. "Can she... can she hear me?"

Skia heaves a sigh and plunks down onto the table, sprawling across the wood and almost knocking over the contact solution. "*When she's listening, she can hear you.*"

"Is she hurt though?" I shut off the water, press my shirt to my arm, and hurry forward. "Is she okay in there?"

Skia waves a lazy black paw. *"She's fine. Annoyed that I'm moving around so much."* They roll onto their back and look at me upside down. *"She'd rather we sit in the sun all day,"* they say with a nod toward the windowsill where Missy's basket sits.

I chuckle and blink away a burning in my eyes. Then I inhale, crack my knuckles, and return to the table. "Hold still this time, okay?"

"I'll try," is the sardonic response.

"Well," I grumble, "we don't want me bleeding all over the place, right?"

"No, it's fine. We need fresh blood, too."

My lip curls in horror, nose scrunched up with disgust. "When were you going to mention that?"

Skia shrugs. *"I assumed you'd be willing to spill a few drops for the cause."*

I grind my teeth, jam the last contact into Missy's eye, and jump back from the table before her claws can dig into me again.

"Right. That's done. Let's get this over with."

Four

A few minutes later, I'm clacking down the rickety stairs with Skia close on my tail. We hurry down four flights, I pull my bike lock key from my pocket, and cross the lobby to the row of bike racks in the far corner.

My footsteps echo across the tile, followed by the soft patter of Skia.

"What is this?"

I halt halfway through sticking the key in the lock. I roll my eyes and scan the bike before I turn to the demon. It's... not really my aesthetic. But it was twenty bucks, has great tires, and came with the lock.

"It's my bike," I rumble out through gritted teeth.

There's a pause. I finish unlocking, pull the bike upright, and walk it to the front door.

Skia hasn't moved from their spot by the other bikes. *"This is how we are getting to the apothecary?"*

"Yes."

Their eyes, a little orange from the combo of yellow contacts and glowing demonic red, fix on the basket. It's white, laced through with pink, purple, and yellow flowers. The bike itself is white—or was before I rode it through the city—with a checkered purple pattern.

"And where am I to sit?"

I gesture to the basket. My lips twitch with the effort of not cracking a grin.

"I'm. A. Demon."

I shrug. "A demon in a cat. If you want to come on the shopping trip, you've got two choices: the basket or my shoulder." I pat my left shoulder, the spot where the real Missy sits when we take trips out of the apartment.

"Ugh," Skia hisses and scurries over. They hop into the basket, turn in a circle, and settle their butt down on the plastic weaving. *"Fine."*

I stifle a snort, push the door open, and hold it with my hip as I roll the bike out.

The sidewalk is relatively clear. The city is large, but it's the middle of the day, and I don't live in the busiest part of downtown. A few people wander by. One smiles at the kitty in the basket and gives me a small wave.

I return it.

Skia hisses.

I swing a leg over, and plant my foot on the pedal.

"Wait."

I heave a sigh. "I thought we were in a hurry?"

"Do you not have protective gear for your brain?"

I cock my head. "Are you concerned about me riding without a helmet?" Incredulity laces my words.

"*I've seen dozens of people fall from horseback and crack their skulls open. Granted, I was often responsible for startling their horse, but still.*"

I chuckle down at the demon. "Are you... are you worried about my safety?"

The response is less of a hiss and more of a growl before, "*Not at all. If you're dead, who will exorcize me?*"

A snort escapes me. I roll my eyes, tighten my grip on the handlebars, and push off. Agatha's Emporium is a dozen blocks away. I know Agatha from college. Her shop is one of the few I visit beyond the grocery store. It's got everything an introvert who hates people could ever need.

We cruise down Main Street for a few blocks, turn onto Elm, and pass the construction site. My peripheral vision catches Skia's head turn every few seconds, taking in the world rushing by.

Something clangs beyond the blue and orange wooden barrier blocking off the work, and the demon-cat nearly falls out of the basket.

"Hey." I reach out and catch their shoulder, gently popping them back into the wicker. "You all right?"

"*Fine.*" Skia glances at me. "*The world is louder than it used to be.*"

I respond with a nod, zipping around a car parked on the wrong side of the street, and slow as we get to a more congested part of the city. Handfuls of people wander the sidewalk. They cluster in the bike lane—idiots—and gawk at the skyscrapers around us.

"Hey!"

I ignore the voice. The person isn't familiar, but the inflection is.

"Hey!" Louder this time as a group of young men leave the bench they were crowding around and approach the edge of the sidewalk.

A low rumble bubbles from my throat as I'm forced to slow even more to avoid running into a group of middle-school-aged children sipping from to-go cups of a popular coffee chain.

There's a jeer.

I stare forward.

One of the men suggests something disgusting and calls me sweetie.

My gut churns.

In the basket, Skia glances from me to the men a few feet from us. The middle-schoolers are out of the way and I'm pedaling again, gaining speed, and leaving the assholes behind. Not in time to avoid hearing them call me a stuck-up bitch.

An inaccurate statement. Bitch and bastard are the defaults, and I'm somewhere between the two. It takes more than three IQ points to come up with a better insult, I guess.

"*What was that?*" Skia hisses as we make a sharp right and come to a quieter, but still touristy block.

I roll to a stop, hop off the bike, and walk it to a set of black ivory twisted doors. An old wooden sign hangs from iron hooks on the brick wall; it reads *Agatha's Emporium* in fancy script.

"Don't worry about it," I grumble, trying to put the moment from my mind and focus on the entirely more important situation at hand.

"*Those humans made you angry?*"

"Yeah," I utter through gritted teeth, chaining my bike up to the convenient post a couple yards from the entrance.

"*I don't understand.*"

"I'm not a..." I heave a sigh. At no point in my coming-out stage did I think I'd have this conversation with my cat. Or a demon. "You get what binary is?"

"*As a concept?*"

"Sure. As a concept. Black and white, right and wrong, one and zero."

"*Heaven and hell, got it.*"

"Cool, I'm not binary. I'm not one or the other of the two options most of humanity uses to categorize themselves."

"*Ahh, yes. I see.*"

I squint at Skia, standing in the basket, surveying me with an unsettlingly intelligent gaze. "Do you actually?"

"*No, but I don't think it matters.*"

I shrug. "Good enough. Let's go."

Skia jumps from the basket and nearly trips me in a very cat-like move of twining around my ankles.

"Stay close to me in here. And don't knock anything over."

The demon hisses. I chuckle. The bell above the door tinkles as we step inside.

Five

Agatha's Emporium is a dark space. Velvet and lace curtained windows, rows and rows of black bookshelves, dangling chandeliers with hints of light, and dark ivy crawling across every open surface. The plants survive on the limited light streaming through the glass door, shadows from the twisted iron designs marring the floor.

The place smells amazing. Always something new but familiar like the changing of the seasons. Pumpkins, cinnamon, nutmeg... I inhale deep, the scents warming my chest. A happy change from the stink of the city and my musty apartment.

Skia sneezes.

I glance down, raise an eyebrow, and open my mouth.

"*Don't.*"

I snort just as Agatha steps out from behind the bar-height checkout counter to the left of the entrance.

"Demi!" She grins and opens her arms. "Hug?"

"Absolutely," I return with a warm smile. It's been a while.

She pulls me in, my arms wrapping around her wide torso, thick curves on curves as she squishes me in a comforting embrace. Her curly purple and black hair cascades nearly to her waist. Fishnet covers almost every inch of skin, long sleeves hooked around her middle finger, a black skirt flaring out around her ample thighs. A dark purple vest buttons just under her breasts, leaving plenty of bosom on display.

"How are you doing?" she asks as she pulls away and bends down to pet who she thinks is Missy. "I haven't seen you in a while. Everything okay?"

"Yeah." I shrug and fiddle with the leathers on my wrist. "Don't worry about me, Ags. I've got my cat."

She rolls her eyes. "And Missy is great."

Skia jerks away from her hands, scrambling around my legs to sit behind me.

Ags raises an immaculately shaped eyebrow. "But you need human interaction, too. Beyond the grocery store."

"I've been getting groceries delivered."

Ags gives me a deadpan stare and straightens. "What's up with Missy? She feeling okay?"

I glance at the demon, currently standing on their back legs as they inspect a ceramic skull on the third shelf of a nearby display. "Yeah, she's a bit off today. Listen, I need to get a few things." I pull the list from my back pocket.

"Didn't come to hang out?" Ags sounds genuinely disappointed, and I offer a sheepish smile.

"Sorry, but I'll come by later in the week to spend some time."

"Lunch?"

I unfold the paper and pass it into her hands. "Sure, that sounds great."

Ags sighs. "I can live with that. You buy—" She falters as her hazel eyes scan the list. "Demi... what is this all for?"

I'm about to attempt an answer when I hear Skia let out a pained hiss. I rush around a bookshelf covered in trinkets and spot them staring at an ornate cross hung above a silver inlaid mirror. I freeze as Ags' footsteps sound behind me.

The thing in the mirror is absolutely not my cat—in a more obvious way than glowing red eyes.

Horns, black and shadowed, rise just in front of dark, elongated ears. Missy's reflection isn't fluffy. Instead, her fur appears short and velvety, a peach fuzz covering pale gray skin. The limbs are long, awkward, and disjoined.

I hurriedly step in front of the mirror, nudging Skia aside with my foot as I mutter, "Be more of a cliché, why don't you," and take the cross from the wall. I set it on a shelf as Ags steps around the corner.

"Everything okay?"

"Like I said, she's not feeling herself today." I turn to my friend and throw on a nonchalant smile. "So, that list?"

The crease in Ags forehead suggests completing my mission might not go well, but she just gives me a squinty, suspicious look and heads deeper into the shop.

"Nightshade and candles I can do. I'll have to double check the back for black chalk."

"*Hmph*," Skia grumbles in my head. "*What kind of magic shop doesn't have black chalk?*"

I wait until Ags pushes through a long black curtain to the small storage space in the back of the store before I round on Skia.

"Knock off the attitude. You should be glad she's helping. And," I shoot an incredulous glare their way, "stay away from mirrors."

Agatha pops her head out from behind the curtain, an eyebrow raised. "Who are you talking to?"

My eyes widen, and I swallow a lump in my throat. "Missy."

Ags sighs. "Human contact, Demi. Seriously."

I flash a tight, toothy grin.

She rolls her eyes and returns to her search.

"*Why does she speak so much of human contact? Are you not contacting enough of your species?*"

I glance at the black curtain before moving toward the front of the store with a gesture for Skia to follow me. I settle onto a plump emerald green armchair studded with gold.

Skia arcs in a nimble leap and perches on a small coffee table to my right. Their tail flicks along the spine of a book sitting on the glass inlaid surface. They tilt their head at me expectantly.

"Humans need..." I grit my teeth. "Humans need to be around other humans. Sometimes. For... comfort and," I blow out a sigh and wriggle in the comfortable chair, "caring. Physical contact is important. Um... conversation. We go a bit crazy if we're alone too long. There's a bunch of studies on solitary confinement that talk about how bad it is for your brain."

"*This seems to be an unfavorable weakness.*"

I blink and gaze at the demon. "Finally something we agree on."

"Demons don't need company. I wandered hell alone for near-ly five decades before I managed to..." Skia darts a look at me as they hesitate. *"Before I came through the gate."*

"Damn. That's a long time. You don't get lonely?"

"Lonely?"

"Yeah. I like being alone, but my life definitely got better when Missy moved in. A warm body around makes the apartment feel less empty."

"Hmm. Hell is warm enough without extra bodies."

I snort, just as Agatha prances out of the back room.

"Found it!" she sings as she strides forward with a double-bagged paper sack. "This is everything on your list. Plus some sticks of cinnamon and pine I just finished drying out. Hang them on a hook and they'll make your whole place smell amazing."

I stand, shaking my head with a smile that creases my eyes. "You're too good to me, Ags." I cross to the check-out counter, pay her, and scoop up the bag. "Wednesday?"

"Don't forget this time. Keep your phone on. I'll call to remind you in the morning."

I offer up a one-armed hug, and she takes it. "I won't. I've missed you."

"You know I don't want to run out your battery, but I do worry about you all alone so often."

I shrug. Skia beats me to the door and paws at the glass for a moment before turning to glower at me.

"I've got Missy."

Agatha shakes her head. "See you Wednesday."

Six

Skia darts out the door as I push it open with one hand, the other clutching my bag of witchy stuff that's supposed to help me exorcize my cat.

"You'll have to ride on my shoulder," I say as I gently nestle the bag into the basket at the front of my bike.

"*No more an insult to my pride than riding in that monstrosity,*" Skia grumbles.

I cackle as I bend to undo the lock and chain.

"Hey!"

My breath hitches. Like a bucket of ice water was upended onto my shoulders, a slam of cold runs down my spine. I swallow, set my jaw, and turn.

The misgendering jerks from before stalk forward from the end of the alley. Just my luck they happen to be passing by right when I leave Agatha's.

My hand tightens around the chain I'm holding. The bike is propped in the metal bike post. I walk around it, listening to the nagging voice in my head telling me not to turn my back on these guys.

With quick fingers, I loop the chain around the seat and pull the bike clear of the pole. The men are closer.

My heartbeat pisses me off. It should be calm. Steady. They're only men.

I glance at Skia. "Hop up. Let's get outta here."

Skia bounds onto the seat and then my shoulder. *"Is everything all right?"*

"Where are you going, sweetie?"

I grimace and say nothing, to Skia or the men now only a few yards away.

I make to swing a leg over the bike. One of the men darts forward and grabs the handlebars, yanking just enough that I stumble and don't manage to get on. Skia slips from my shoulder with a soft yowl. They land on their feet and circle my ankles again.

"Let go of my bike," I growl.

"Aww, come on, honey. You don't need to be like that. I just wanna talk."

My flesh crawls. The scowl on my lips grows, the furrow in my brow expressing my fury and discomfort. Not that they care.

"Ha." Another of them laughs. "Since when do you go for guys?"

"What?" Confusion flashes across the face of the one holding my bike. He looks at his friend, then back at me with a curled lip. "Aren't you a girl?"

"I'm neither, asshole. Let go of my bike."

The air shifts. A weight comes down as their faces change, warp as confusion and malice replace the fun time they thought they were having before.

The one holding my handlebars yanks again, and my grip on the seat slips. He shoves the bike over. It clangs to the ground. A bundle of green falls from the top of the paper bag, a few pieces of orange and black striped tissue paper are picked up by the breeze.

He steps forward, and I square my shoulders, raising my jaw.

His hand slams into my sternum. I hit the wall behind me with an oomph and a grunt.

"Back off," I manage through gritted teeth.

My ears ring. Whatever they're saying—they're all talking now, words pouring out and trying to weigh me down like wet cement—I can't hear them. All I hear is the pounding of my blood and my breath.

The man's mouth moves, utters something inconsequential as he pulls back a fist, and I brace for the swing.

He freezes.

I blink and step to the side. He doesn't move. I step again, my gaze sliding from his immobile form to the men behind him.

They aren't moving either. Their mouths are open, curses and insults hanging on their breath.

Then I notice their eyes.

Their eyes *are* moving. Wide and terrified and...

I take a step forward, squinting for a second before I stumble back in horror.

Black oozes from their eyes. Tears of darkness, stinking of sulfur, drip down their faces and fall to the ground. The asphalt sizzles.

"What..." I breathe.

"***That was a mistake.***"

I know Skia's voice isn't only echoing in my head, because the eyes of the men around me widen even further. I glance at the demon cat. They've changed, morphed Missy's body to look more like the creature I saw in the mirror. Not quite that level of terrifying, but definitely not a cat anymore.

The ground shakes. I take a few steps back, putting the wall at my back as Skia deliberately circles the men.

"***One you will pay for... with your lives.***"

The guttural hiss with which Skia speaks sends fresh chills down my spine. One of the men breaks from his paralysis and falls to his knees with a whimper. He wipes at his eyes and lets out a sob as his fingers come away coated in black ooze.

"Skia," I murmur, sure they can hear me even as the wind picks up around us, the ground groaning and shifting. "They don't need... I think this is enough for them to learn their lesson. You don't need to kill them."

"***Need?***" Skia looks back at me, that angular body disjointed and sharp. The contacts fell out with the transformation, and their red eyes glint with unnatural light. "***Who said anything about need? These men ought to die simply because I wish it.***"

The one on the ground screams and scurries to his feet. Panting and sobbing, he races to the end of the alley, stumbling on the cracked, uneven asphalt.

"Skia," I say again, my voice soft against the roaring earth and air. "Let them go. This isn't right."

"***Let them...***" Skia falters. Their form shrinks as they look to me. "***They hurt you. They wanted to hurt you more.***"

"But they didn't. You stopped them."

The form shrinks more, becoming the tiny black cat I recognize. "*I did.*"

"Thank you."

Skia give a slow blink, the red of their eyes disappearing for a long second. When their eyes open again, whatever holds the men in place breaks. They scatter, leaving behind a scent of fear and piss.

"*You're...*" Skia swallows and gives a swish of their tail. "*You're welcome.*"

"What the hell was that?"

I wheel around. Agatha is standing at her shop, the door propped open, a phone in her hand. Her eyes are round, fear on her face.

"Uh..." I glance at Skia and bend to pick up the things that fell from my bike basket. I tuck them into the paper and lift my bike off the ground.

"I called the cops, Demi. Those guys..."

Her gaze darts to Skia, then back at me.

The fear on her face has shifted to something different. Excitement. Curiosity.

My mouth twitches up into a smile. "Like I said, you don't need to worry about me. I've got my cat." I jerk my head at Skia. They take three looping steps, jump onto the bike-seat, and then to my shoulder.

I swing my leg over the bike, wave to Ags, and begin to pedal us home.

Seven

I take the long way back: narrow alleys, no tourists, limited people. We pass a few unhoused persons, a cop, and a lot of trash. I make a sharp turn only a few blocks from my building and zip down a dark street. Light shines on a two-lane thoroughfare at the end, but the buildings on either side of us are too high for any sunlight beyond an hour in the middle of the day.

We're maybe twenty yards from the T intersection at the end of the alley when the air shudders. Warps. I slow to a stop, heartbeat racing.

"Was that you?"

Skai swallows, the sound audible as their throat is right next to my ear. "*No.*"

I wait, jaw tight and back tense. There. Where sunlight meets the shadows, the ground begins to sink.

A pit of molten rock stretches out, maybe five feet in diameter. Hooked sludge-green claws grasp the edges.

The heavy weight of fear drags at my stomach, pulling me down, rooting me to the spot.

"*No, no, no,*" Skia mutters, trembling on my shoulder.

"Skia, what's..."

Words leave me. Thought leaves me as the creature before us pulls itself from the ground. The long, narrow claws connect to insect-like arms, bent in three places like a spider with an extra joint. Almost as many of them, too. It plants five claws onto the asphalt and lifts its body.

Bile builds in my throat.

As dry and skeletal as the arms are, its lumpy body drips with sludge—a familiar black ooze that sizzles where it falls on the street. The head is mangled. Six eyes—that I can see—two at the front, two on each side. Not human, not by a long shot, but not insect either. Maybe similar to a rat, with the elongated nose and pointed teeth, but the ears are twisted up like a candy-cane. Like something gripped the ends with pliers and spun them in circles.

It looks beyond painful.

Then again, maybe those aren't the ears. As fear curdles in my belly, sending shudders down my spine, I note black slits between the sets of eyes. Maybe the things on its head are horns.

"*Foolish thing.*"

I exhale a breath of terror. This thing doesn't speak like Skia, a soft murmuring hiss in my head. This thing's words echo, reverberating through my skull and sticking to the walls of my brain with painful burs.

"*Do not speak,*" Skia's voice follows, so quiet compared to the thing before us.

"*Thinking you could escape? Leave your place?*"

The being approaches, leaving the sunlight and stepping onto the sidewalk. Its claws click against the cement. The pit behind it shrinks and disappears.

"*I did not escape, Nexus,*" Skia says.

I don't know if I'm supposed to hear this, too. A car drives by. A woman walks past on the far side of the street. Confusion ripples through me. Why do they not stop? Stare? Scream?

I'd scream. If I could make my throat work again.

"*I slipped out while you were busy. Didn't want to bother you."*

The response is one of spitting fury. White glints in the thing's—Nexus's—eyes. Pinpricks of light in the bulbous shining black spheres on its head.

"*How dare you? I have been the gatekeeper for a thousand-thousand years. You were **forbidden**, little shadow.*"

I wince as the words slam into me. *Little shadow,* said with such derision, scorn that my throat starts working again only to utter a furious growl.

Skia's tail strokes down my back, shooing some of the fear from my spine.

"*I'm not going back, Nexus.*"

"*You'll go back, shadow. You're not meant for freedom. You're meant for the pits of hell, just like the rest of us. I will pry you from that horrid form as slowly as the Drakons skin a sinner. And when we get back home, you will learn pain well enough to stop you from making such a mistake again.*"

It steps forward, each of the five claws scratching the ground. My mind clicks now, forming thoughts beyond the situation at hand. Ahead of it. Trying to figure out if I'll be able to swing the bike around and gather speed before Nexus is on us. Passing it is out of the question. Those legs... I don't want to know how long they reach when fully extended.

"You can't escape me. Not on those weak, bipedal legs."

I barely have time to blink in confusion before Skia hisses on my shoulder. An audible, out-loud hiss as their claws contract, the pressure comforting against the fabric of my sweater.

"You will not touch the human," Skia snaps.

There is a pause. A hesitation as the dots of white in Nexus's eyes flick from me to Skia and back to me again. I shudder.

"Oh." A chuckle, sharp and chilling as wind ripping across an icy surface. *"Ah, I see. Oh, shadow. What a failure you are. Though perhaps that beasty is fitting for you. A small thing. Worthless."*

Fury slams into me. Hot and fierce, a flame against the frozen fear I've felt since Nexus emerged from the pit. Skia coils against my neck.

My lip curls in a snarl. "Shut up."

"It speaks? Brave..." The rat-like head tilts, a glob of ooze falling to the ground and leaving a rutted dent in the sidewalk. *"Do you know what we do to the 'brave' in hell, human? We scrub the rough edges with sandpaper until all the brave is scraped away, and the only thing left is smooth fear."* Its nose lifts into the air and sniffs. *"Delicious, tender fear."*

I put a foot on the pedal, readying myself to swing around.

Something slams into Nexus. There's a flash of green, white, and flailing legs as the insect-like demon flips in the air and lands on its back.

"Damnit, Trent!"

My jaw drops, and my eye twitches as another rent-a-scooter rolls over one of Nexus's outstretched legs, loses balance, and falls to the side.

A build-up of scooters, demon body-parts, and young men in kaki pants and polos, clumps on the sidewalk where the alley meets the road.

"It wasn't me, Cody." The guy on the first scooter scrambles to his feet, sandals flapping against his heels. "The scooter got tripped up on something."

"There's nothing for it to trip up on but your yeti feet," another snaps.

Their conversation fades to the back of my attention as Nexus utters a sigh in my head, twitches, and fades into smoke.

"*We have to go. Now.*"

I nod, flip the bike, and pedal us toward my apartment. "What was that, Skia?"

"*Nexus. Keeper of the sneeze gate.*"

"Sneeze gate?" I repeat with less amusement and more incredulity.

"*There are many ways to enter your world, Demi. The sneeze gate is one. The most active one at times.*"

"Why, exactly," I huff, pumping my legs until they burn and taking turns far faster than I normally would, "is the sneeze gate keeper after you?"

"*It is possible that I did not get the authority of my superiors before... uh... slipping through the gate.*"

"You—" huff— "snuck—" huff— "out of hell?"

"*When you put it like that... yes.*"

Eight

"What just happened?" I ask after I've slowed down a little, giving myself the ability to breathe again. "Did those guys destroy that thing?"

"Not in the slightest. Nexus was momentarily tangled, and likely thought shadowing out was the fastest way to get himself undone."

"Why did..." I gulp, glancing behind us for the twentieth time as I turn onto our street. "Why could I see it—him, and no one else could?"

"Because he thought I was in you. Had he known my form from the start, it's unlikely he'd have let you. Demons do not like being seen by mortals. It puts them on their guard."

"You can say that again." I slow to a stop at the door of the apartment building. "Do you..." Skia jumps from my shoulder. I use my keycode on the door, push it open, and follow the demon inside. "Do you look like that?"

"Nothing so fierce." Skia glances back with a somewhat sheepish expression on Missy's face. *"Shadow demons are the smallest of our kind. My true form is... petite."*

If I wasn't still scared out of my mind, I'd laugh. As it is, a smile crosses my face. I heft the paper bag and make for the stairs, Skia on my heels.

My phone rings halfway up. It's Ags. I send it to voicemail and put the ringer on silent. I will call her. After I get Skia out of my cat.

I fumble with the lock, fingers still trembling from our encounter.

"Okay." I set the bag on the shoved-aside coffee table. "What now?"

"Start by drawing the shapes I gave you with black chalk across the floorboards."

"How long..." I get my notebook and the sticky notes and quickly draw the complicated lines Skia explained before we left. "How did he find you?"

"I was foolish."

"That doesn't answer my question."

Skia hisses, smudges a section of chalk with his padded paws, and directs me to redo it at a slightly different angle. *"I used my demonic powers. They can be traced."*

"Will he be able to tell when you go into someone new?"

"I... I'm not sure. Nexus did not come here. He did not know I was in this form. I believe I have to use a deeper power for him to track me."

I finish off the chalk circle with a flourish. "No pentagrams?"

Skia rolls their eyes. *"Not everything hellish needs a pentagram, Demi."*

I shrug. "So we get you out of Missy, you enter a different body, and... what? Nexus just leaves?"

"Once you are no longer harboring me, Nexus will be unable to harm you without facing severe punishment in hell. I believe when he has lost the trail, he will return to his post."

I pause in the middle of placing nightshade in little clusters around the drawing. "You believe? What if he doesn't leave?"

"He will leave."

"How do you know?"

"Because when you send me back to hell, he will follow."

I freeze. Heat goes through my chest. "What do you mean, back to hell?"

"He's found me. When I'm in a larger, more capable form, it will be harder to hide my demonic powers."

"Your powers are limited by the cat body?" I set the candles out.

"Infuriating, isn't it?"

"But you don't have to go back, do you? I thought we were just doing the first half of this. You'll find a different body."

"At my most powerful, I might be able to fight Nexus and survive. But beating him? Out of the question. Besides..."

Skia's tail swishes. They nudge a candle half an inch to the left.

"Besides what?"

"If I stay in this realm, it is possible Nexus could make a claim that you are still... caring for me. You have to send me back."

I open my mouth to argue, but a strange scent hits my nostrils. The stench of rotting meat, blown through the open window.

I rise and walk to the sill, leaning out just enough to see the sidewalk on the busy street below.

A shudder races down my spine. I jerk back and slam the window closed, fiddling with the little lock a moment too long before it finally slides into place.

"*Demi?*"

"He's here." My mouth is dry. My fingers shake. I run across the small apartment to the door and slide the chain across.

"*That's not going to stop a gatekeeper from hell, Demi.*"

"Better than nothing," I snap.

"*Start the ritual. I will do what I can.*"

Nine

I frown at the cat-demon and return to kneel at the edge of the sigil. Fresh blood is the last thing, beyond the words I have to sound out.

I gulp. I don't like pain. Never have, never will. No masochists over here.

I pick up the cheese knife I cleaned before we left for Agatha's. My hand quivers over my arm.

Something slams into my door.

I nearly fall over. Eyes wide, my gaze darts to Skia—standing a few feet from the door and staring at it with furious intensity—before I pierce my skin. Blood drips, too slowly. With a wince and a moan, I widen the gash a few inches from my wrist on the top part of my arm.

I toss away the blade. Blood dribbles now. Enough that I can dip two fingers into the red sludge and trace the symbols that require it.

Another slam against the door.

I jerk back from the sigil, grasp for a strip of gauze I laid out earlier, and wrap it around my arm.

Then I lift my notebook off the floor and begin to read.

The words come slow, halting, and thick on my tongue. I don't speak this language. The words are written so I can read it aloud.

I have no idea what I'm saying.

"*I can't hold him much longer,*" Skia hisses. They step back. Once, twice, a third time until their back legs are at the edge of the chalk outline. "*Once the first part of the incantation is done, Missy will be free from me. Keep her out of the circle. If she steps in during the second half, she might be sent with me.*"

An ache creeps through my chest as I nod, hesitating. I've reached the last few lines of the first section. Skia backs a little further.

The door cracks. A jagged hunk of wood chips off the center. Nexus's long, sharp teeth glint through the opening.

"*Finish it,*" Skia says.

I do.

The air picks up. Wind swirling through the apartment, though none of the windows are open. The candles flicker but don't go out. The flames grow, rising two, three inches from the wicks as rumbling fills the space.

Skia—Missy—yowls in the center of the sigil.

I scramble back, the notebook clenched in my fingers as I press against the wall bisecting my apartment. Nexus continues to pound on the door, but my gaze is stuck on my friends.

Harsh sounds fill the air: ripping, tearing, scratching. Softer ones as well; a whimper, a cry.

Missy darts from the sigil, brushes by my ankle, and disappears under the pushed-aside loveseat.

There, left in the center of the chalk and blood and candles... a tiny black shadow.

Skia's form *is* petite. About Missy's size, even a little smaller. Darker than night, but warm. Like the coals left over after a fire burns out.

They open their eyes. The same glowing red that stared at me through Missy stares at me now.

"Are you..." I don't know what to ask. Are you okay? Are you sure about going back to hell?

"*Finish it,*" Skia snaps.

The same voice, still whispering in my head.

Missy yowls from under the couch.

The door splinters open. Wood slams against the wall, one of the hinges cracks, and the door hangs off its side.

Nexus stalks into the room; his nails click against the hardwood floor.

A shudder runs down my spine. I lift the notebook and continue the ritual. Only three lines left.

Missy yowls again and crawls out from under the couch.

Two lines. My throat is dry.

Say the name. That's the important part. Make sure you say the name...

One line left.

Missy's familiar yellow eyes meet mine.

Nexus approaches. Looms over Skia.

They shrink inward. Wince away from the claws reaching out to drag them back to hell.

Nexus spares a glance at me. A pitiless, bottomless black gaze that drills me to the spot.

Missy yowls one more time—launches off her hindlegs; I say the last word, and everything goes dark.

Ten

Swirling black smoke consumes my apartment. Shrieking, endless voices screaming, flames and ash lick up from the sides of a pit in my living room, growing to the size of the sigil.

Nexus stands over the pit. Confusion fogs his eyes. The ground before him trembles as it sinks inward. There's a split second of time as he looks around for his prey.

His claw, about to sink into the shadowy form of Skia, now hangs over empty air. Across from me, pressed against the wall, is my little cat.

Missy, having leapt from her place by the couch as I uttered that final word... her body covering the demon.

Nexus screams. Shrill and violent and terrible as he falls, grasping at the sides of the floor for traction. But none is found.

I said his name. I did the ritual correctly. Even if there were chains binding him to the room, he'd still be sinking into hell.

A moment passes and the screaming fades. The floor closes up. There's a mess of chalk, blood, and candle wax, but no pit to the abyss, so I'm gonna call it a win.

"*What...*" Skia slides out from under Missy. Their movement is fluid, gliding across the floor. "*What did you do?*"

I brush back the sweaty hair clinging to my forehead and take a deep breath. "Well, you said the name is the important part. He only found you cuz you used your powers. It's not like he knows the mortal plane very well..." My eyes go wide with a moment of panic. "Right? He said it had been thousands of years. He doesn't like... know what street we're on, does he?"

"*No...*" Skia stares, from me to Missy and back again.

Missy pads up to them and rubs her back against their shadowy form the same way she does to my ankles.

"*Why did you do that?*"

I swallow, finally pushing up from the floor as I stride across to the mangled front door. I glance back at them. "Why did you stop those guys from hurting me?"

"*I...*"

The shadow seems lost for words. Their red eyes narrow, no eyebrows to furrow or expression to read, but they stutter for a moment before falling silent.

"Listen," I say, pitifully scraping the door closed. A new one won't be cheap, but if I can get Ags to help, I might be able to install it before the landlord finds out. "I get that you wanted to find a new body to possess, but you also said that's a good way for Nexus to find you."

Missy approaches as I turn to face the room. I bend and scoop, cradling her in my arms. She puts a paw on my shoulder and rubs her head against my chest.

"I was thinking..." I swallow, scratching behind her ears. "If you want to, that is... but you might stay with us for a while." I gesture at the wreck of an apartment before Missy puts her paw on my hand and drags me back to giving her scratchies. "There's plenty of room. I can get some blackout curtains for the windows if you need dark places to be during the day or something."

"You'd... continue to harbor me?"

"Sure. You're not the worst company. And Missy clearly likes you."

Missy purrs in my arms, wiggles, and launches off of me, landing lightly on the ground. She flicks Skia with her tail as she makes her way to the windowsill. A moment later, she's back in her usual perch, curled up and enjoying the sun.

I chuckle. "We are gonna have to tell Ags about you. I hope that's okay. She's been calling me nonstop since we left the shop." I pull my phone out. It hasn't stopped vibrating since I turned the sound off. "You okay if I tell her to come over?"

"I suppose... I suppose that would be fine, as long as she promises to leave her crosses at the store."

"I don't think that'll be a problem. In fact, I bet once she meets you, she'll take them down permanently."

"Why?"

"Because she's gonna like you as much as I do. And that's the kind of thing you do for a friend."

· · · ● ● · ● ● · · ·

A week later finds the four of us at my apartment. Chinese food containers litter the kitchen counter, the smell of egg foo young being aired out via the open window.

Missy sits in her basket, content and seemingly unfazed by her short stint as a demon's body.

Ags and I laugh at the table, cracking open the dozen fortune cookies we got from the restaurant. The front door is fixed. A new hunk of wood in place, complete with a few sigils burned into the bottom.

Skia sits on their own perch at the top of the wall covered in plants, munching on an egg roll. The greenery offers enough shade that they don't get uncomfortable from all the light. They are a shadow after all, and shadows don't last long in the sun.

The apartment seems bigger these days. Pockets of darkness hide my new friend during the day, and at night they can't seem to leave the window. Just the sliver of sky visible from our spot on the fourth floor is enough. They stare at the stars until the sun comes up.

Ags and I are planning a trip out of the city in a little while. We could use a break from the traffic, the noise. Let Missy run through some tall grass. Let Skia see the sky without all the light pollution.

I meet Skia's red eyes with a wide grin and toss up another spring roll. A tendril of black shadow grasps it out of the air.

I lean back in my chair, my gaze falling briefly on the scab across my arm. A small price to pay. One I'd pay again.

After all, that's what you do for a friend.

Thank you!

I hope you enjoyed reading this as much as I enjoyed writing it. Find book two, One Hell of a Road Trip, and book three, Spelling Disaster, out now!

www.ingramcontent.com/pod-product-compliance
Lightning Source LLC
Chambersburg PA
CBHW061553310726
48972CB00008B/2736